I0727072

BORN AGAIN

WRITTEN BY JOHN WARD

Edited by Kacey Flynn.

Published by Arbutus Studios (www.arbutusfilms.com).

Cover image by Get Covers

Book design and layout by Vestan Pance

ISBN: 978-1-7383580-4-5
eISBN: 978-1-7383580-5-2

CONTENTS

For Maggie and Oskar.

Born Again

The metal and glass monolith towered over its modest west-side neighbours. Its myriad windows reflecting so much moonlight it was practically a lighthouse, a beacon of gentrification visible for all to see. A crow circled it before perching on a streetlight at the farthest end of the street. It cawed as the light beneath it began to flicker and then went dark. The same thing happened to the neighbouring streetlight, then the next and the next; each dying as a wave of darkness rippled towards the glass tower.

Moonlight poured through the floor-to-ceiling windows of Becky's tenth-floor apartment illuminating the modest but tastefully decorated interior. The furnishings were slender but sturdy, each hand-crafted and designed specifically for the 800 square foot space, transforming the claustrophobic box into an open and roomy home. The decor flowed smoothly from the kitchen to the living area and down the hall towards the master bedroom where Jason Collins lay on the queen sized bed beside his sleeping wife. He had woken from a dream, but the images rapidly faded leaving him with nothing but a vague sense of dread, and the restless realization that sleep was now beyond him. Softly and silently he rolled off the memory foam mattress, naked aside from plaid pajama pants. He hurried towards the door only to stub his toe on the bed-frame. Stifling a scream he pogoed on one foot until the pain dissipated and then hobbled out, soundlessly closing the door behind him.

Jason limped across the polished wooden floor and into the kitchen. The microwave clock cast an eerie glow indicating it was a hair after three am; the hour of the wolf. He turned on the espresso machine which roared to life with a prolonged howl. As the water filled the reservoir he rifled through an abandoned hamper nearby. He promised Becky he would take care of the laundry but had somehow never found the time. Reaching for a t-shirt, he gave it a quick sniff before throwing it on. He then poured a long, dark espresso and carried it into his office.

The space was technically classified as a second bedroom, although given its size he wasn't sure what the builders were thinking. He had been excited by the prospect of turning it into a space of his own: a fortress of solitude from which he would bang out prestigious novels and screenplays. But now - five years later - the room overflowed with racks of dresses, skirts, and blouses and he was relegated to the darkest corner with barely enough room for a fold-up desk. He knew it could be worse: at least he didn't have to go back to writing in coffee shops where failure clung to him like a nasty stench, invisible yet detectable by anyone who came close. At least now his failures were private, known only to himself and the contents of Becky's walk-in-closet. He sank into the cheap office chair, fired up his MacBook and took a sip of espresso as his latest half-finished masterpiece flashed on screen. He typed a sentence, stared at it for a moment and then deleted it. He took a sip of espresso and searched for inspiration in the darkness, and then began typing again, only to delete everything once more.

THUNK.

Someone pounded on the apartment door.

He was so surprised it took him a moment to react to the noise, but then leapt to his feet and spilled coffee down his pants. He hurried out of the office, cursing under his breath as he massaged his gently scolded crotch. The pounding continued, rhythmic and loud. Jason feared it would wake Becky, she had another big day in court tomorrow and needed her rest. He stormed towards the door, preparing to unload on the obnoxious caller, but his bravado evaporated with each subsequent step, and it was with meek trepidation that he finally peered out through the tiny keyhole in the door.

"Holy shit." Fear prickled his flesh. He steeled himself, unlocked the door, then threw it open.

"Hey man it's good to see you — how you doing? You look well — Keeping fit? You go to the gym? I go to the gym all the time — I can bench 150 pounds these days. 150 pounds. Bet you can't do that." Anders' voice boomed with the power and speed of an out-of-control freight train. He was an imposing sight at the best of times - a hulking, two-hundred pound, six foot white guy with waist-length dreadlocks, an out-of-control beard and tattoos covering every inch of his arms. Today... today was something else. He was drenched in blood from head to toe. His dreadlocks were matted with chunks of unidentifiable gore. "What's up, man — you look like you've seen a ghost?!"

Jason pulled him into the apartment and shut the door. "The hell are you doing here?" He whispered.

"Demons — that's why I'm here, yeah? I need your help so we can send them back to hell or wherever they came from — maybe it's a parallel dimension or something? You know about that, right? You're the physicist. Branes? D-branes? You're the one with the brains." He laughed at his own joke.

"How'd you find me?" Jason kept his voice low, hoping Anders would pick up on the hint and do the same.

"Kara told me — she said you'd help me if I asked you, so I'm asking — can you help me?"

Jason stared at his friend. He tried to imagine a scenario to account for his blood-drenched state, but could only conjure images from his most persistent nightmares.

"Jason? Is someone there?" Becky was awake.

"Take a shower," he whispered to Anders and pointed the way to the bathroom. "I'll take care of her." He scooted to the master bedroom and slipped inside.

Becky was awake, but still lying under the covers. "What's wrong?"

He quickly moved to sit on the edge of the bed beside her. "It's okay. It's okay. It's just Anders."

She sat up and flipped on the beside lamp. "The drummer from your band? What's he doing here?"

"He's wasted. He needs somewhere to sleep it off."

"And he came here? When was the last time you saw him? Five? Ten years ago?"

"It's been a while," he shrugged. In truth it had been eight years, but he didn't want to give her such an easy victory. Anders was his oldest friend. They had grown up together. They had gone to school together. They had skated together. They had been in a band together. They weren't blood but they were as close as brothers. They were bonded by words and deeds that he couldn't even begin to explain to her, especially at this time of night. Or they had been.

"Where is he?" Becky threw the bedsheets aside.

"Taking a shower. I already told him he could crash on the couch."

"I don't want him in my apartment."

"He's not dangerous."

She paused. "Why would you say that?"

"Because… he has schizophrenia. Sometimes he can be a little prickly and that can scare people."

"So you've invited a drunk schizophrenic to sleep on my couch?"

"Our couch."

"That's not the fucking point, Jason." She was angry. He could tell by the twitch of her eyebrows twitched and the subtle flaring of her nostrils. "It's three in the morning. I have a big case tomorrow and the last thing I need is another deadbeat disrupting my sleep."

"I'll take care of him." He retreated to the bedroom door.

"Jason?"

He could tell Becky wasn't buying it. He could almost hear the cogs whirring in her brain. "I'll take care of it. Get some rest." He exited and closed the door. He half-expected Becky to emerge behind him, but it remained closed.

He heard someone rummaging in the fridge and drifted into the kitchen.

"Where'd you get this tracksuit? It's dope." Anders closed the fridge door. He had scrubbed up and was now squeezed into an old lime-green tracksuit that Jason had purchased but never worn.

"I don't remember." Jason turned to the espresso machine. "Coffee?"

"Nah, man — I don't drink that stuff — gives me an upset stomach so I try to avoid it — I drink tea though — herbal tea, like chamomile or peppermint or hibiscus. You got any tea? I'll take some tea." Anders rummaged through the cupboard and found a box of granola, which he proceeded to stuff handfuls of into his mouth. "I'm hungry — can't remember the last time I ate."

"You gonna tell me why you're here?"

"Right, right, right. You know that gardening job I've been doing — maybe you don't? I dunno. I don't get paid to do it, it's kinda voluntary — but I like that it's peaceful and I get to be outside — I really like working Three Oaks — it's a care home for old people — they're a riot. There's this one guy — Dave or Daniel or something — he used to play drums in a band too. They were a ska band I think or maybe they were reggae? Or two-tone? I can't remember and I think it was years ago —"

"I'm sorry," Jason was confused. "Is this part of the story?"

"Right, right. Yeah. You know, sometimes I get side-tracked. Sorry about that — yeah, I was talking about Three Oaks which is my favourite place to work — until I discovered it was over-run with demons — they'd taken over the staff and were feeding on the old people. Like eating them. Sucking souls from their corpses and fucked up shit like that. That's where I was tonight. I went there to try and save them, but..." he trailed off.

"What?" Jason had expected some kind of story, but certainly not that. He frowned at Anders, scanning his face for signs it was a joke. There was no humour in the expression that met his own. Jason sighed. He nodded to himself as the realization crept up on him. Anders had gotten worse. He clearly needed help, but what could Jason do? He was a writer, not a therapist.

"They're all gone, man — there was so much blood, there was nothing I could do."

"What does this have to do with Kara?"

"How'd you know about Kara?"

"You told me."

"I did? Shit. I don't remember, man. There's too many voices in my head — sometimes it's hard to keep everything straight." He yawned.

"You know she's dead, right?"

"I know," said Anders. "But that's the fucked up part, man. One day she was just there. I could hear her, talking about the old days. She told me lots of things and they've all come true. She sent me to Three Oaks tonight and helped me stop the demons — then she told me I needed to come and see you. We have to find this guy — Douglas something — they're coming for him next and we're the only ones who can save him."

"Who's coming for him?"

"The demons." Anders slammed the box on the kitchen counter and walked away.

Jason followed him, unsure what was happening. "Anders?"

Anders shuffled into the living room and collapsed onto the couch. He yawned. "I'm just telling you what she told me — I don't know what the fuck she's talking about half-the-time but I listen because she's always right — the demons are real, man — I saw them and I saw what they did and I can't stand by and do nothing." He looked down at the ground.

After a few moments Jason broke the silence. "Are you okay?"

There was no response. Concerned, Jason stepped forward to check on him.

Anders snored gently. His eyes were open but he was definitely asleep.

Jason considered waking him but decided against it. He skittered to the bathroom and returned with a large white blanket. He carefully lowered Anders onto his back and placed the blanket over him. Anders snored softly but his eyes remained wide open. Jason had never seen anyone sleep with their eyes open before. He wasn't sure it was even possible yet here was the unfortunate proof. He thought about going back to work but decided against it. He drifted back to the master bedroom and quietly slipped inside.

***

Jason carefully positioned the glass tumbler beneath the spout and watched it fill with aromatic brown fluid. It was a single espresso kind of morning.

He couldn't remember the last time he slept so soundly. Usually he woke multiple times, with the echoes of nightmares reverberating in his mind. But not last night. He slipped back into bed and into a delirious slumber. Truth be told, if Becky hadn't been so persistent with her shaking, he would probably still be asleep. She had left the apartment in a hurry, saying nothing about the events of the previous night, but slamming the front door on her way out to remind him of her displeasure. He knew they would end up having a conversation about it later, but for now he didn't care.

He turned off the espresso machine and transferred the hot beverage into a glass cup that had recently been soaking in a heat bath. He took a long sniff as he brought it to his lips, and savoured the first luxurious sip.

Hearing a noise from the living room he drifted over just as Anders was rousing.

"You want coffee?"

Anders shook his head. "I'm good. Thanks, man. Everything okay?"

"I'm fine. Why?"

Anders shrugged. "I wanted to say thanks for last night — I know I haven't been the best at keeping in touch — turning up out of the blue like that — must've been a surprise."

"You could say that."

"But I meant what I said," Anders continued. "I need your help to find Douglass Wendall — I understand if you can't come — I can be a lot to deal-with at times, but I'm not crazy — I know what happened last night, and I know what Kara said, and I need to stop it from happening — I know you don't believe me. I can see it in your eyes. But that's okay, I'm used to it. I just want you to know that I'm many things, but I'm not a liar. This shit is real, man."

Jason sipped his coffee.

"I know we haven't been close these past few years — and believe me, I wouldn't have come here if there was any other way — but you're the only person left I can trust."

"Is this about money?"

"I don't need your fucking money, man — I need you — I can't do this on my own. For one thing they won't let me drive — but Kara told me to come find you — she needs us to do this together — she always said you were the best guy she had ever known and there was nothing you wouldn't do for her."

"You need help," Jason shook his head. "Did you forget to take your meds or something There's no such thing as demons."

Anders was crestfallen but tried to shake it off. "I get it. It was good to see you, man." He headed for the door.

Jason felt the heavy weight in his chest. "Wait."

Anders stopped but didn't turn around.

"Where are you going?"

"You know where I'm going — I have to find this guy. You might not believe me, but I'm sure he will." Anders opened the door and stepped into the hallway. He closed the door behind him.

Jason was alone in the apartment.

Becky's apartment.

He felt small. Vulnerable. Isolated. He wanted to help, but didn't know how. Anders was his best friend. His only friend. He wasn't himself. Or maybe he was? His heart and mind raced with all the possibilities. He was moving before he was aware of it. He grabbed the car keys from the bowl on the counter, pocketed his phone, and snatched a coat from the rack before heading out of the apartment, letting the door slam in his wake.

***

The homestyle diner was empty save for the middle-aged woman nursing a cold coffee at the table closest to the bathroom. Jason had suggested they stop for a rest. The drive had been long and gruelling. They had talked a great deal at first, catching up on their lives and reminiscing about the past, but as the kilometres ticked off the silence became more frequent and was soon as thick as the mountain mists that surrounded them. The landscape, previously flat and welcoming, was now rugged and threatening, and thick forest tendrils grasped for them through the soupy-mist. The road that wound through the mountains was little more than a collection of potholes forcing Jason to drive with extreme caution. After hours behind the wheel his body and mind needed a rest, which is when he spied the lonely diner, half-devoured by the rainforest canopy and set back some fifty yards from the road.

"This reminds me of that time we played in Blaine — remember that shitty road though the forest when we went the wrong way and almost went into that ditch — that was such a great show though, the crowd were so into it. Remember?"

"Yeah." Jason sighed. He sat opposite Anders in a small vinyl booth, a half-eaten meal on the table before him. In truth he didn't remember most of their shows. His memories of those years had merged into an amorphous blur, and most days he didn't even remember he had been in a band. Worse, when he did remember, the memories were uncomfortable; unwanted intrusions from a past life he had long discarded. "You sure you know how to find this guy? You have his address or phone number or something?"

"Chill, man it's all good — you need to trust me on this — not everything is black and white and easily quantifiable, sometimes you need to take a leap of faith — recognize there's a bigger plan.

"Did we lose faith when we almost drove into that ditch in Blaine? No fucking way — and ultimately if we didn't make that wrong turn we never would've found the venue. Things always happen for a reason, right?"

A slither of recollection flickered in Jason's mind. "Wasn't that when the engine caught fire and we had to call Kara's dad to come pick us up?"

"Yeah. He got stuck at the border crossing and turned up at five in the morning with coffee and cinnamon buns."

"Good times."

"Great fucking times."

They basked in the warm glow of the shared memory, but slowly the smiles faded and uneasy silence returned.

Jason carefully dipped fries into a small pot of ketchup and tossed them into his mouth. They were hot, crunchy, and salty, just the way he liked them. Or used to. Becky suggested they should eat more healthily, which he had discovered was code for eating more salad. Fries, like so many other things, had vanished from his life. He glanced over at Anders' untouched plate. "So are we close?" he spoke between bites.

"Close enough," said Anders.

Jason sensed that was all the information he was going to get. For whatever reason, this was something Anders didn't want to share. "Can I ask you something? What really happened last night?"

Anders turned away in disgust.

"Come on. You can trust me. I mean, I'm here aren't I? I just want to know what we're dealing with."

"You won't believe me, so what's the point?"

"Humour me."

Anders stabbed one of Jason's fries with a fork and stuffed it in his mouth. He chewed slowly. "I already told you."

"Demons?"

"See? I knew you'd react that way — you think I'm making it up — or worse; maybe I hurt people and imagined they were demons. I am schizophrenic after all."

"No that's not what I was..." he trailed off. Truth be told, the thought had crossed his mind.

Anders snatched the burger off Jasons' plate and bit into it, spraying mayo and ketchup all over the table. "If you believe I could do something like that then you should turn me in. I'm a danger to the public — I could do anything to anyone at any time — isn't that what your wife was afraid of?"

Jason sank back in his seat hoping it would swallow him.

"I wish I could tell you what happened, but I can't — I don't really know — it's like an intense dream that lingers after you wake up — you only get snapshots — an image here a sound there — sometimes things happen that are impossible to believe — you try to wrap your head around them, but the words don't make sense — you know what I mean?"

Jason shook his head desperately wanted to believe his friend but the story sounded more improbable with every passing minute.

"You didn't believe Kara either," said Anders as he licked greasy fingers. "You re-live that conversation every fucking day, turning it one way and then the other — wondering what could've happened if you had believed her — maybe she'd still be alive — maybe I wouldn't have been pushed into a breakdown — maybe the two of you would've... I dunno — maybe things would've turned out different for us all?"

Jason's voice cracked as he spoke. "Conversation? What conversation?"

"You know which one," said Anders with a mouthful of ketchup-stained fries.

Jason's heart pounded.

He felt light-headed.

The room began to darken. Jason felt the walls closing in.

Was he having a heart-attack?

His own father had died of a heart-attack just a few years ago, and he morbidly wondered if their experiences were the same.

"I need some air." He staggered to his feet and rushed for the front door, not slowing until he was half-way across the parking lot. He finally paused near the Prius to catch his breath. It had been years since he had felt panic like that. He took long, measured breaths of the damp mountain air, closed his eyes, and the tension in his chest slowly eased.

His phone buzzed in the pocket of his jeans. He removed it and spied a notification from Becky. He had almost forgotten about his phone, given there was practically no reception in the mountains, but now he saw there were two signal bars, although one continuously flicked in an out of existence. He opened the app and was confronted by a list of unread messages. His eyes focused on the most recent: U OKAY? He instinctively started to respond but stopped himself. What exactly was he going to say? That he was on a wild-goose chase with his delusional best-friend? That he was lost somewhere in the mountains and just wanted to go home? No. He couldn't say those things. He couldn't give her the satisfaction of being right again. He needed to see this through to the end; whatever that meant. He deleted his response and closed the app. Instead he opened the browser and searched for information on Douglas Wendall. The colour drained from his face as he read the search results, and the pain in his gut returned with a vengeance.

Jason burst into the diner, phone in hand - but Anders was nowhere to be seen. He looks around, but there was no sign of him. He sank into the vinyl seat, feeling the weight of his discovery. This couldn't be a coincidence, he saw that now. This was calculated, but he had no idea what game was being played, or who was playing it.

A foul stench wafted in from the open bathroom door. He covered his nose with his sleeve as Anders calmly trotted back to the table.

"When were you going to tell me?" Jason slid his phone across the tabletop. "Douglas Wendall was a child abuser. They came for him the same day they arrested Colin. Says here they were part of the same pedophile network. They knew one another."

Anders didn't seem fazed. "I know. Kara told me.

"You knew and you didn't fucking tell me? Why did we really come out here? Was this about revenge? Did you want to find him to get even with him?"

"You think I want to be here? You think I want to save this fucking pervert? If it was up to me, I'd let the fuckers have him — but it's not up to me. It's up to Kara, and she told me I need to save him — we need to save him."

"Fuck this." Jason hurried out of the diner and headed for the Prius, pulling the keys from his pocket and steeling himself for the solitary drive back to Vancouver. He was barely aware of Anders following him.

"You don't get to walk away, Jason — you're part of this whether you like it or not."

"I should've listened to Becky. I've enabled this fantasy for too long already."

"Kara told me about the safe."

Jason stopped. His feet wouldn't move. He urged them forward but they had merged with the concrete beneath him. He couldn't even turn, and could only stare ahead at the parked Prius taunting him from three feet away.

"You should've told her when you found out what was inside." Anders continued. "If you had, she might still be alive."

"I didn't see it. Not really. I was only there for a second before Colin came in. He swore the photos weren't his. He said they belonged to a friend. He said he was going to turn him in."

"You let yourself believe him. You looked the other way because it was easier. All you had to do was say something — anything — and everything would've been different."

"I didn't know what would happen." Jason could feel tears welling.

Anders positioned himself between Jason and the Prius, and for the first time Jason felt a twinge of fear as he stared at his friend. "That's why you need to help me. You owe me. You owe Kara. You owe it to yourself, man — I'm not having some crazy fucking episode. I know she's gone — but I can still hear her, whispering to me, guiding me — she needs us to do this together. You can't fix your mistakes. None of us can. But we can atone for them in the here and now — that's what I'm asking for. That's what she's asking for. You let her down so many times when she was alive. Are you going to let her down again?"

Jason fought back the tears. He didn't want to cry in front of Anders. His insides ached. He had worked hard to forget all about Colin and the safe. Over time he had managed to create a false narrative — one that finally helped him sleep at night, one that allowed him to come off the medication and start a new life, one that had allowed him to let down his defences enough to meet and connect with someone like Becky. Anders words ripped through that illusion like a laser. "No," was all he could muster as warm tears finally streamed down his face.

***

The lonely farmhouse lay several kilometres down a winding, long-abandoned logging road, nestled neatly into the mountains and surrounded on all sides by thick forest, making it invisible from the highway. Jason and Anders parked the Prius and covered the last kilometres on foot, as the sun sank below the tree-line.

Their conversation had been sporadic since the diner with neither entirely sure how to re-engage. Jason let his mind drift as they walked down the middle of the road, hypnotized by the crunch of small stones underfoot. Memories of Kara and Anders flickered into view, random flashes from long-forgotten shows in smelly, sweat-filled basements, Kara's dad lingering at the bar watching them play.

Anders unexpectedly broke the silence. "The first time I heard her voice I thought I was having a stroke — I knew she was gone — I knew what I was hearing was impossible — but at the same time it was comforting to hear her again. For the longest time I resisted — I ignored her and tried to push her out of my head — but she kept coming back — she kept telling me things and one day I stopped resisting and listened. But I'm scared, man. What if she's not real? What if she's just another hallucination like the others?"

He paused, his brow furrowed as he tried and failed to find an answer to his own question. "I see a therapist, but she doesn't understand — she's not interested in what the voices tell me, she just wants to drug me and keep me quiet. I think she's afraid of me. Everyone is — except you."

Jason slapped him hard on the shoulder.

Anders smiled and nodded.

The house loomed before them. A dirt path ran from the road to the front door, and given the tire tracks it functioned as a makeshift driveway. A thin plume of smoke rose from the misshapen chimney, barely visible against the pale grey sky, and flickering lights danced in each of the windows. A trio of crows cawed from their rooftop perch, watching them with curious interest as they crept up the dirt path, passing an old black Ford truck. Jason made a beeline for the front door but was pulled back by Anders.

"Where you going man? You're gonna knock on the door and ask the man living there if he's a wanted pedophile who's living off the grid to avoid the authorities?"

Jason was a statue. Of course that had been his plan, but Anders was right. In that instant, he realized how naïve he had become, how his life was safe and comforting, unpolluted by thoughts of monsters. He realized he was badly out of his depth and wanted nothing more than to head home, even though he knew it meant another argument with Becky, but he had come to far now to simply walk away.

"We don't even know who else lives here — let's check the place out before we do anything stupid."

Jason followed Anders around the side of the house. There were plenty of windows offering numerous opportunities to peer inside. Through these portals, the interior overflowed with aged and worn furniture, giving it the appearance of a junk shop rather than a home. A tired and sagging couch dominated the living room, positioned directly before the large wood-burning hearth. Mismatched tables and chairs were scattered randomly and there was a lack of television — or any other electronic devices, for that matter.

A shadow swept down a hallway. Jason flattened himself against the outside wall. His heart pounded as he heard a man's muffled voice calling to someone.

Anders motioned for Jason to move to the next window. They peered inside.

The man loitered outside a closed door with his back to the window. The hallway was lit entirely by oil lamps which cast strange flickering shadows on the wall, but there was sufficient light for them to note the man's black jeans, black sweater and his long and unkempt hair. He was about to knock on the door when it opened and a young girl pushed past him, evading his clumsy attempts to grab her. She dashed down the hallway, vanishing into the interior of the house.

"Zoe!" The man pursued the young girl. She was barely a teen. Lean in a non-athletic way and wearing clothes that hung from her frame.

"Is that him?" Jason whispered. Hearing no response he turned. Anders had already scampered to the next window. Jason followed and glanced inside. The man had the young girl up on his shoulders. She laughed raucously, her hands wrapped tightly over his eyes. It was Wendall. There was no doubt about that. He was older and thinner, but the man before them was the same one Jason had seen in the photos back at the diner.

There was a yell and a young boy, no more than 12 years of age, rushed into the fray and tickled Wendall's belly with a large fluffy brush. He laughed heartily, drawing the attention of a dark-haired woman who could only be Zoe's mother. They were almost identical, sharing high cheekbones, and the same wild, raven-black hair which the woman wore in a bun. She stood to the side, watching the trio wrestle for a few moments before joining the tickle-fight.

Jason watched, absorbing the sounds of raucous laughter as they wafted into the darkened sky, but finally he had enough. He turned away, his back firmly pressed to the exterior of the house. The surrounding forest seemed much closer than he had initially realized, with swaying branches barely a few feet from his face.

Anders left first and Jason followed. They walked quickly away from the house, keeping to the edges of the road, staying silent until they finally saw the Prius up ahead.

"Maybe we should call the cops?" Jason ventured. "They're probably still looking for him. We could tip them off and they could pick him up."

"They can't save him from what's coming — we're the only ones who can."

"So why don't we just tell him?"

"Just like when I told you?"

Jason stopped. "So what's the plan? You keep saying we have to save him, but what exactly does that mean? You shoot down every idea I come up with but don't offer anything in return. What if I say no? What if I say I don't want to help? What will you do then?"

"I'll do it on my own." Anders walked on, striding past the Prius, and heading back towards the distant highway.

"Fine with me." Jason climbed into the Prius and slammed the door. He was tired and didn't need this shit. He turned the ignition but nothing happened. He tried again. Same result. He glanced in the rear-view but Anders had already disappeared, swallowed by the darkness.

Something pinged off the hood.

There was nothing visible through the windshield but he heard the agitated scream of a nearby animal. He tried the ignition and this time it caught. Third time's the charm, he thought. He revved the engine and the soft purring noise helped put him at ease. He threw on the high-beams and made a sharp turn, driving away from the house and back towards the highway. He drove slowly, scanning the road for any sign of Anders, but saw nothing. He was confused. Anders couldn't have gotten this far could he? With every few feet, the doubt began to seep in. He wondered if Anders had doubled back and gone back to the farmhouse.

Something stepped out in front of the vehicle.

Jason slammed on the brakes. He stopped mere inches from Anders, who barely seemed to register the near impact. Jason threw open his door and stepped out. "Jesus. Are you okay?"

Anders turned and walked away.

"I'm just tired. It's been a long fucking day and I need some sleep," Jason said. "Please get in the car. You want me to beg? Please."

"Please."

"Please."

"Please."

"Please."

Anders stopped. He slowly turned. "We passed a motel a few kilometres back — we could stay the night there and come back in the morning."

"Okay." Jason didn't want to argue.

Anders shuffled back to the passenger side door and got inside. "Let's go."

Thirty minutes later, Jason opened the door to the motel room and flipped on the light. The lone bulb bathed the cramped space in a dark and unsettling orange hue. He arched his eyebrows, took in the twin-sized bed that was squeezed between the window and an oversized oak dresser. He had seen worse; had stayed in worse, but that had been a long time ago. His tastes these days were significantly more refined.

Anders closed the door and flopped onto the stained white comforter. "Sick," he said, but then jolted and sat upright on the edge of the bed and looked around, startled. "You hear that?"

Jason listened. He heard nothing but an unusually loud electric hum. "What?"

Anders got to his feet, eyes fixed firmly on the stucco ceiling. He shuffled towards the door to and studiously examined the high corner. "Guess it was nothing."

Jason locked the front door and kicked off his shoes before collapsing on the bed. He rotated his body so his feet were close to the headboard, grabbed a pillow and stuffed it under his head. He lay down and closed his eyes.

"Just like old times," said Anders as he returned to the bed and lay down. "You ever wonder if these old places are haunted? There's probably ghosts in every room — like that one place we played at in Whitehorse. Remember?"

"Go to sleep," said Jason.

There was a noise and he opened them again. It was daytime. The room was bathed in early morning light. Jason sat up, alarmed. The motel door was wide-open and there was no sign of Anders.

"Anders? "Jason drifted outside into the cool morning air, his bare feet crunching on soft gravel. He looked around but saw no-one. He carefully hobbled out to the Prius and checked inside, just in case. But the car was empty. There was no sign of life anywhere. Anders had gone. But where?

Jason thought for a moment, and then the answer slapped him with its simplicity. "Shit." He rushed back to the motel room to grab his shoes.

***

Jason hurried down the logging road, desperately gasping for air. Each January he vowed this would be the year he would finally hit the gym, but his resolve would only last as long as the dry weather, and evaporated on the first rainy-soaked morning, which was invariably the next day, more often than not. Right now, it was a decision he regretted, and silently promised himself that he would start to get in shape the moment he got back home.

He heard the crows before he saw them. They circled overhead, cawing at his unwanted incursion. They dive-bombed him, strafing his sweaty head with their claws, and then nestled in the branches along the road, hissing at him. After what felt like an eternity he finally turned into the makeshift driveway and made his way towards the farmhouse.

The truck was missing. It took him a few moments to realize it, but then it occurred to him that it was a good thing. Maybe they had gone out? Maybe Anders was outside somewhere, lying in wait?

He bounded towards the front door and tripped on a carelessly placed shovel, he stumbled but somehow managed to keep his balance, then raced up the warped wooden steps and onto the porch. He slammed his fist against the weathered wooden door. "Hello?" he yelled, as he struggled for breath.

There was no response. He knocked again

There was a sound from inside which reminded him of a metal object scraping against wood, and to his surprise the door opened — just a crack — as Wendall peered out from the dark interior. "Can I help you?" His voice was soft and quiet, and almost threw Jason.

"Oh hey. Sorry to bother you. I'm looking for my dog, Hank. You seen him?" The lie rolled so easily from his tongue it almost seemed real. "Traffic was snarled up pretty bad and he jumped out the window. He's a German Boxer—"

Wendall threw the door wide open.

"Sorry to hear that," he said, a look of genuine concern on his face. "I haven't seen any dogs, but I'd be happy to help you find him."

Jason struggled to respond. His throat felt tight. Words flickered in his brain but couldn't coalesce into a coherent expression of thought. He hadn't expected to see Wendall up close, and certainly hadn't expected the warm and congenial response he received. He opened his mouth, hoping the act alone could summon a coherent sentence, when he heard the sound of an approaching vehicle. Wendall's eyes flickered.

Jason turned and watched the black truck bounce on the uneven surface as it approached the house. It stopped and the rear doors flew open as the two kids leapt out. "Dad," the boy shouted as he made a beeline for the porch, his sister shuffling behind him at a more glacial pace.

Wendall received the young boy and wrapped his arms around him.

"Zoe's being a B-I-T-C-H this morning."

"Don't say that about your sister."

"It's true."

Zoe climbed the steps to the porch with a look of disdain on her face. She made eye contact with Jason and he withered under her penetrating gaze. Her blue eyes sparkled like an azure mountain lake, but never blinked. Not once. Jason wanted to turn away but found himself paralyzed. "I'm going to my room," she muttered as she stepped inside.

"Who's this?" Eleanor shuffled up the steps, her muscular arms strained under the weight of six overflowing grocery bags. She was shorter than Jason recalled from the previous evening. Her hair was wrapped in a functional but spirited ponytail, and she wore a pink shirt that clashed awkwardly with her olive-coloured yoga leggings.

"M-M-Mike," Jason stammered. "I'm Mike. I was looking for my dog and thought he may have come up this way."

Eleanor climbed the stairs with no effort. She held out two of the bags to her son. "Take these inside, Tommy?"

"Mom."

"Thomas!"

Sensing dark menace in her tone, Thomas reluctantly took two of the bags and struggled inside. Eleanor handed two more bags to her husband. "Sorry to hear about your dog."

"Thanks," said Jason.

"We were just going to look for him," said Wendall.

"Of course," said Eleanor. "Let me get this stuff put away and I'll help too." She stepped over the threshold, pulling Jason into her gravitational wake. "We don't get too many visitors out this way." She led him down a rustic hallway lined with closed doors. Another closed behind him.

Jason casually noted the strange stone figurines on the few tables lining the hallway. They were about the size of a fist, and extremely crude in design, but were somehow strangely alluring. He had never believed inanimate objects possessed an energy, yet these figurines gave him pause. There was something ancient about them. Something dark and terrible. Something familiar that lay just out of reach.

"Kitchen's down here." Her words echoed all around him, even though he had lost sight of her.

"I don't want to put you out." Jason stumbled blindly through a nearby door and into the massive kitchen. The space was dominated by a large wood-burning stove; beside it was a hand-made countertop upon which balanced various pots, pans, and an ancient kettle. A propane-powered fridge-freezer stood in the corner, the most modern appliance he could see.

Eleanor placed her bags on the countertop and stooped to pick up the two Thomas had left on the ground. "Would you like some tea?" She already had the kettle in hand and filled it with water from a makeshift tap.

Wendall stepped around Jason and also placed his bags on the countertop.

"We don't get many visitors out here," she repeated. "It's a rare, but pleasurable occurrence, isn't it babe?"

Jason kept his eye on Wendall, who busied himself putting the groceries away.

"How did you know?"

He turned back to Eleanor and saw the large kitchen knife in her hand. The blade glinted as she stepped towards him.

"Know what?"

"Babe?" Wendall was genuinely shocked.

"Don't play games. Who else knows you're here?"

She knew.

He spied the quiet, determined rage in her eyes. He had once seen the same rage reflected back at him in his old bathroom mirror. It was an anger fuelled by revelation, one that could lead even the gentlest of souls towards destruction. She knew about Wendall. That much was obvious. She knew what he'd done, but had somehow come to terms with it. From her perspective he understood he was now a threat, not only to her husband, but to her entire family.

"Everyone. My wife. My family. Lots of people." Jason gulped.

Eleanor smirked "You're a terrible liar. I'm guessing no-one knows you're here. Am I right?" Her voice was cold. Her eyes were dark. Jason shrank back as she advanced on him.

"Ellie, what the hell are you doing?" Wendall was confused. He hadn't moved an inch from the countertop; a flat of eggs still in hand.

"How'd you find us?" She asked. "We've been so careful all these years."

Jason felt the wooden door at his back. He struggled to find the handle.

Something struck the door from behind him. He was flung forward by its propulsive momentum. A fast-moving blur raced past and struck Eleanor. She screamed and collapsed to her knees, the kitchen knife planted firmly in her stomach.

The blur was Zoe.

Zoe pulled the knife from her mother and then stabbed her repeatedly, eviscerating shirt and skin until she tore through muscle and intestines.

"Ellie!" screamed Wendall.

Jason couldn't move. He stared at the horror unfolding before him, hearing the discordant screams but unable to get his legs to function.

Zoe dropped to her knees and tore into Eleanor's throat, chewing on the sinewy flesh. Unspeakable gore dripped from her jaws as she stared first at Wendall, and then turned her attention to Jason.

Adrenaline surged through his body. Finally he was moving. His legs carried him away from the bloodbath and back down the hall before he even realized it. As soon as he became aware, he tripped and fell to the ground.

Zoe was on him. She flipped him onto his back like he was a doll, and slashed at him with the knife. He somehow kept her at bay with his long, spindly arms, but she had incredible strength and he knew he couldn't hold her off for long.

"Need a hand?" Anders grabbed her by the waist and lifted her into the air with his powerful arms. She kicked and thrashed as she struggled to free herself.

Jason scrambled to his feet. Every part of his being urged him to run, to get out of this house and never look back. But he couldn't. He felt something solid in his hands. He didn't recall grasping for the statue, but he swung it all the same. The blow caught Zoe in the side of the head and she went limp. Anders dropped her to the ground and her knife skittered across the hardwood floor.

"Thanks man," Anders was barely out of breath.

"We have the to get the fuck outta here!"

"Not without Wendall. Where is he?"

"Who cares?" Jason backed away. "We gotta go."

"We can't. We owe Kara." Anders headed back to the kitchen.

"Fuck!" Jason rushed after his friend.

The two men stood in silence and stared down at Evelyn's eviscerated corpse. There was no sign of Wendall.

A man's muted scream bled through the ceiling, and they both looked at the worn plasterboard above their heads. Anders bolted, leaving Jason alone with the twitching corpse. He fled, rushing down the hallway in pursuit of his friend.

Bounding up the rickety staircase, he followed Anders down the second floor landing towards the master bedroom as the screams began in earnest. They found Zoe standing on the threshold of the room, with her back to them. "Why didn't you ever want to fuck me, Daddy? Was I not your type? Was I too old for you? Was I not sexy enough for you?" She laughed.

Anders charged at her.

At the last moment she turned, grabbed him by the throat, and tossed him aside She turned her attention back to the room. "Give him to me."

"Zoe. What's happening to you?" Wendall's voice trembled with fear.

Jason helped Anders to his feet. From this position he could see into the room and spied Wendall standing between Zoe and Thomas.

Zoe grabbed her father and tossed him up at the ceiling. He collapsed to the ground in a heap, screaming as something snapped beneath him. "Now you want to touch me? Too little, too late, Daddy."

Anders rushed forward and punched her in the face.

Blood erupted from her broken nose.

She smiled, bearing her blood-stained teeth.

Anders tackled her to the ground with a triumphant yell.

Jason edged forward and held out his hand for Thomas. "Take my hand." The boy shook his head, he was scared out of his mind. Jason understood. He was too. But it was now or never. Jason rushed forward. He grabbed the boy, lifted him over his shoulder and beat a hasty retreat, trying to ignore the violence raging behind him.

They burst out the front door. Thomas was heavier than he looked and Jason felt his arm-muscles burning, but he couldn't put the boy down until they were clear. Finally his boots hit the driveway and he released his burden. Thomas immediately turned to rush back inside and it took everything Jason had to restrain him.

"Daddy," Thomas stopped struggling.

Jason looked back as Wendall hobbled out of the house, beaten and bleeding, but otherwise in one piece. He released the boy who raced into his father's outstretched arms.

"Why are you fighting me?" Zoe was him, blocking their path to freedom. She snapped her fingers and a large crow landed on her left shoulder and nuzzled her with its beak. Despite what he had witnessed, her nose looked fine. In fact she didn't have a single hair out of place. She stoked the crow's back with genuine affection. "We both know what he's done, and yet you're trying to save him. Why?"

"What do you want?" Jason stammered.

"What do you want?"

"What?"

"Why are you here?"

"Demons?"

"Wrong answer."

The voice came from behind him. He turned and saw her standing beside Thomas, the crow in hand. She snapped its neck and stabbed her brother in the neck with its razor-sharp beak.

"No," Wendall screamed. He reached out for his son, but Zoe knocked him aside and dragged the bleeding boy further away from the house. "Time to rest now, Tommy." She dropped the boy's corpse to the ground.

Wendall collapsed. He wailed.

Despite his better judgment, Jason positioned himself between Wendall and Zoe.

"Step aside," barked Zoe.

"I can't."

"Why? Because you made a promise to some dead people? Step aside. Go home to your comfortable life. Forget about this place. If you don't..." She snapped her fingers.

Thomas sat bolt upright and in one unnatural motion managed to pull himself directly into a standing position. He blinked and looked around. His eyes were dark and dull, just like Zoe's. He met Jason's gaze and broke into an impossible smile.

Creak.

Jason turned to see Eleanor shuffling down the stairs behind him. Crows flocked to the gaping hole in her chest and pecked at the gizzards. Eleanor barely noticed. Her eyes were also black holes aimed squarely at Jason.

"Last chance," said Zoe.

Jason grabbed Wendall. He tried to lift him to his feet, but it was hopeless so he violently shook him. "Get up. I can't carry you."

Wendall was unintelligible.

Jason looked around. He spied the shovel that had almost tripped him earlier. As a weapon, it looked useless, but it was better than nothing. He had come too far to turn back now, no matter what. He turned to Eleanor, spinning the shovel in his hand, and then Thomas and finally back to the advancing Zoe.

Zoe shook her head and smirked.

Creak.

Anders leaped from the porch and tackled Eleanor.

Jason could've screamed. His heart soared. Anders was still alive. He raised the shovel and turned to

Thomas. "Stay back," he warned. Thomas reached for him and Jason swung. The shovel decapitated the child just above the shoulders, showering Jason in a tsunami of viscous black bile. His stomach revolted. He bent over and spewed acrid phlegm and vomit.

"You were always weak." Zoe grabbed him by the throat and lifted him into the air. "It's no wonder she turned you down all those years ago. She saw just how pitiful you really are."

He didn't panic. Even as he felt his windpipe being crushed, he remained calm. He still had his hands on the shovel and slowly raised it, sliding his hand down the metal shaft. He swung at Zoe with everything he had, smashing her hard in the head. Her grip weakened and he dropped nimbly to the ground. He swung again. Then again. Each swing landing with terrible fury, cleaving a large hole in her skull and showering him fragments of bone and brain. He didn't stop. He smashed her skull like it was a piñata. He didn't stop even as she flopped to the ground, her legs spasming with each shattering blow. He didn't stop until he felt a hand on his shoulder.

"Hey. It's over," said Anders.

They looked down. Zoe's head was little more than a bloody pulp, covered in sticky black fluid that bubbled and frothed as it seeped into the ground below. "This is officially the worst-fucking road-trip of all time," Jason said.

Anders pulled him in for a long hug, which Jason was slow to accept. When they came, the tears were thick and fast. "Sorry," he wiped his eyes. "It's just a lot to deal with." He opened his eyes and discovered he was alone.

Jason looked around, assuming Anders was playing a game. "Anders? Hey. This isn't funny." There was no response.

"Kill me." Wendall lay curled up on his side, rocking rapidly.

Jason scanned the area for his friend but allowed himself to be pulled in.

"Kill me," Wendall repeated, his voice raspy and cracked. "Do it."

"What are you talking about? We came here to save you."

Wendall burst into laughter. It was an unsettling sound; the sound of someone whose mind had finally broken.

Crows cawed, mimicking the strange vocalization. Jason watched three of the beasts land on the corpses and pick over the softer flesh.

"I know who you are. You looked familiar, only I couldn't place you. Now I remember. We met once. Briefly. You were friend's with Colin's kid. You were in that fucking band." Wendall was strangely coherent.

Jason felt his stomach turn.

"Terrible what happened to her. Being arrested like that. Being accused of pimping for her father. I can only imagine how hard it was when they let her go. People don't care about facts. They had already made up their minds. I bet they made her life hell - at least for the few days she let them." With a grunt, Wendall pulled himself into a seated position. His eyes burned with agonizing pain and his voice was frail and weak. "You know, I always thought suicide was a coward's way out."

"Shut the fuck up."

"Make me."

For a split second he considered it.

He fantasized about pounding his fists into the ashen face.

The moment passed. Reason returned. He knew he was being goaded.

"Where's Anders? You see where he went?"

"Who?"

"Anders. Big guy with dreads?! We helped save you."

Wendall cocked his head.

"He was just here."

"We're the only ones here. We're the only ones left."

Jason felt unsteady on his feet. His skin crawled. His pulse raced. His throat tightened. "What are you talking about?"

"Are we going to do this or not?"

"I'm not a killer."

"Not a killer?" Wendall laughed once more. "I deserve to be punished for the things I've done. I know that. But my wife... my kids... they didn't deserve that. They didn't deserve to die."

"They were demons. They were trying to kill us."

Wendall stared at him. The furrows in his brow deepened. "You're fucking crazy. You're just like Colin's kid. She was crazy too."

"Shut your mouth."

"She knew about her old man, you know that? She found a bunch of photos in his safe. Stupid prick must've left it open while he was pleasuring himself.

He caught her snooping, but convinced her not to say anything."

"How — do you know — that story?" Jason struggled to find the words. His legs were suddenly jelly. He couldn't move, all he wanted to do was collapse to the ground in a heap.

"Colin told me. One night. Beer always loosened his tongue, it was what made him a liability. So are we going to do this? Are we going to finally end this?"

Jason shook his head. He was frozen. His eyes stared beyond Wendall as long-forgotten memories danced behind his eyes. "It wasn't her — she didn't find the safe. I did — I was the one who promised Colin I wouldn't tell. He said they weren't his — he said they would take Kara away if anyone found out — he begged me to keep it a secret until he could fix things. I shouldn't have believed him — but I did — the band was all I had, and if she was taken away..."

"So it was you? Well, I guess this is your chance to make things right. Kill me. Do it you piece of shit. Do it. Do it. Do it."

Jason found the courage to turn and flee. He raced down the driveway, Wendall's words ringing in his ears alongside the nauseating call of ravenous crows. He needed to get away from the abattoir. He needed to get home. He needed to get back to Becky; back to his unfinished novel, back to his unfinished life.

He didn't stop until he was safely back at the Prius. He sat in the driver's seat for a long time and just stared through the windshield, pondering what had just happened. So many questions. So few answers.

A crow landed on the hood and cawed, snapping him back to reality. He noted its red-tipped beak and claws. He turned the key in the ignition and the engine spluttered to life. Sensing the danger, the crow abandoned its post and flew into the forest, leaving a bloody print on the white hood. The Prius lurched forward and then made a U-turn before speeding back towards the highway.

***

He stopped briefly at the motel to shower and change his clothes, discarding the blood-stained apparel in separate garbage containers before hitting the road. The surrounding forest cackled with crows, presumably summoning their brethren to the dark feast.

It was dark by the time he made it home. He left the car in the underground parking stall and rode the lonely elevator to the tenth floor.

"I was worried sick." There was anger in Becky's voice as she hugged him. He didn't care. He was happy to be home. "Why didn't you answer your phone?"

"Battery was dead," he said, burying his face in her silky hair and sucking in a lungful of its fruity scent.

"What happened to you? I was going to call the police."

"Long story," he said. "I'll tell you all about it once I've had a shower."

She looked down. She had bad news.

"What is it?" He asked.

"I'm sorry. Anders has passed. They found him in his apartment two nights ago. The police said he'd been dead for at least a week. I wanted to tell you, but you weren't answering your phone."

Jason's head throbbed. His eyes were unable to focus and he had the distinct impression he was falling.

"I thought you were talking to him the other night? Isn't that what you said?"

Jason didn't know how to respond.

A massive weight pinned him to the ground, crushing his rib cage and forcing the air from his lungs. He gasped and sputtered but couldn't catch his breath. The carpet pulled at him, sucking him into the material with its fibrous tendrils. He resisted. He tried to lash out but his limbs were limp and unresponsive. In his mind, Zoe's face appeared before him and he broke down. Anders had said she was a demon. She had attacked him. She had killed her own mother. He had seen it happen with his own eyes.

Right?

Right?

Doubt seeped into his mind and he began to drown in a raging torrent of his own anxiety. Had he gone to the mountains with his friend? Had they fought off demons?

Becky pulled him out. She was above him, looking down with concerned and empathetic eyes. The darkness vanished at her touch and he realized he was lying on the floor of their apartment. She knelt beside him, terrified and fearful.

"It's okay — I'm okay," he sputtered, unsure if he truly meant it. "I'm okay." He caught something moving in his peripheral vision and turned to better see it.

Through the window he saw a crow perched on the ledge. It peered into the apartment and made eye contact. It cawed.

***

Jason sat at the keyboard typing furiously.

He had heard about being in "The Zone" from other writers but had never been there himself. He wasn't sure if he was there now, but the words flew onto the page with such ease that he really believed it. The music helped. It was loud and obnoxious yet soothing in its own way. He wasn't listening to it. He had heard the songs a thousand times; had written most of them before they went to the studio. Becky hated it of course, and refused to enter the room while he listened. Demonic music was how she described it. He didn't care as long as it gave him uninterrupted writing time, especially when he was writing so forcefully like he was right now. He paused and breathed warm air onto his cold hands.

"This book isn't gonna write itself man — you know that right?" Anders voice was crystal clear in his mind, so clear it was almost as if he were in the same room.

Only he wasn't.

He was dead.

Jason had devoured the reports with his own eyes and had spoken with some of the officers who had found Anders' body. Suicide was the official cause of death, which made Jason almost vomit when he read it. As for Wendall, there had was no news. He spent the first few days expecting to see something, and jumped every time he heard a siren, but as the days passed he began to relax. On some days, he could almost forget what had happened, and on the other days, he heard Anders' voice from the shadows, reassuring him that he was safe, and reminding him that even if Wendall had gone to the authorities, no-one would believe him.

Jason wanted to believe, but couldn't. Not fully.

He rubbed his palms together for warmth — it was always cold in this room, no matter how high he turned the thermostat — and returned to his story. His fingers clattered the keyboard and the white page rapidly filled with black text. The trip had done something to him. He was transformed. He now slept through the night and his writing had become ferocious and undeniable. An agent had already signed him to a three-book deal and a hefty advance sat untouched in his bank account. The weight he had felt in his being was no longer there.

He paused at the end of the paragraph and leaned back in the chair. "Slaves to Mammon," blared from the Bluetooth speaker on the table. It was pure thrash-core; blast beats and heavily de-tuned distortion that supported Kara's strangely beautiful vocals. Above him on the wall, their first album poster hung in pride of place. A gift — one final gift — from Anders. The image was crudely drawn in scratchy black marker but depicted a silhouetted woman birthing a demon; the band's logo —Born Again — arced above her in barely legible typeface. Jason paused to stare up at the central image.

He had never before noticed how the woman on the album cover resembled Kara.

A
CONFESSION

Dearest Daniel,

'Tis twilight and time is running short. Two loathsome creatures stand guard outside my window, tapping their beaks on the glass to remind me of their dark presence. As if I could forget. I have procured most of the necessary supplies for my upcoming voyage, but anxiously await the return of my maid who ventured into the storm in search of plum cakes. Where am I going, you may ask? Nowhere you wish to venture, dear Daniel, but I hope all will become clear once you read this final letter. I ask you not to mourn, but to task yourself with finding all the copies of my accursed book, and to burn them in a raging inferno.

As you undoubtedly recall, I spent much of my early years collecting folklore and was particularly taken with Brand's "*Observations of Popular Antiquities,*" and – of course – the magpie verse which remains forever etched into my memory.

One for sorrow.
Two for mirth.
Three for a funeral.
Four for a birth.

What you do not know is that the final three lines identified in my own work were bestowed upon me through a brief, but unforgettable, encounter with Mister Jonathan Balls in late 1846, an encounter I must lay bare in order to be compliant with scripture. If you are unfamiliar with Mister Jonathan Balls, I urge you to review his story in any of the Norfolk newspapers, at is a truly sad and disturbed one. He was posthumously accused of murdering over a dozen friends and family members through poisonous means. In truth, he confessed to me that the number was closer to one hundred, and that he was compelled to take their lives in order to save more.

But I get ahead of myself.

Mister Balls was an avid fan of my early work and, upon discovering I was in Norfolk for work, he sent word that I should join him to discover the warning behind Brand's verse. I admit to being somewhat flattered by his interest, and soon found myself in his derelict and dark abode. Although the newspapers waxed lyrical about his broad and muscular stature, the man who greeted me that day was thin, and wan, with barely the effervescence to greet me, and he quickly retreated to a makeshift bed of dirty rugs in one corner of the filthy living room. Beside him, I noted a holy bible, a selection of silk handkerchiefs, several plum cakes, a fire iron, and a pair of coal tongs - which was strange as there was no signs of fire in the hearth. We made polite conversation, but it was stilted and confusing, until a solitary magpie made landing upon a ledge outside the window and pecked the glass. Almost immediately Mister Bolton sat upright, his countenance changed, and he began to expound his narrative with increasing rapidity, pausing only to cut a large wound into the flesh of his arm as he spoke the words "one for sorrow."

He had – he confessed – been responsible for the murder of a large number of persons in order to save humanity. He claimed God had ordered him to defeat the armies of Satan as they tried to establish a new Hell onEarth. Initially, he told me he had been skeptical of the voice's provenance, but over time had come to see the truth - that Satan's minions were hidden amongst us and only through acts of violence could they be returned to the pit.

At that point, a second magpie landed beside its companion and they began to alternate their knocking. "Two for mirth," saidMister Balls, as he carved a second sigil beside the first.

Sensing my piqued curiosity, he explained that he would soon be dead, for Satan's eyes had fallen upon him and would soon come for his soul. But – he went on – he didn't fear Satan, as an ancient scripture had showed him the path to Heaven; all he needed was to confess a secret and obtain a collection of charms to be placed with him in his coffin. He implored me to see to this action upon his passing.

Two more magpies landed on the ledge and joined the atonal chorus. "Three for a funeral. Four for a birth," said Mister Balls as he carved two more fiendish marks on his arm, letting blood pour to the floor. He sank back into his blankets, weakened by the blood-letting, and increasingly haunted by the corvids' relentless knocking.

"Brand misunderstood the purpose of pie counting," he whispered. "It no more wards off evil than throwing salt. The true purpose of the count is to summon the dark one, himself."

At that juncture, two more magpies joined the crescendo, and the unearthly cawing and knocking edged towards syncopation.

"Five for heaven. Six for hell." Mister Balls carved two more marks into his arm, which was now a bleeding mess of skin and bone. The pain alone should have made him scream, yet I do not recall him raising his voice even once.

"Why would anyone choose to summon Satan?" I enquired, growing increasingly uneasy by the moment.

"No-one of sane mind, that's for sure." He replied with a wink. "Not unless it was their only chance to escape eternal damnation."

A seventh bird landed.

"Seven for the devil…"

The window shattered inwards, spraying us with deadly shards of hardened glass. The wind howled as a frenzied white and black cloud burst forth into the room. The creatures descended upon Mister balls, stabbing and piercing him with their beaks and razor-like talons.

I confess, I threw myself under a nearby table and screamed for God's mercy as I watched the beasts eviscerate their prey, tearing him apart piece by bloody piece, burrowing into his corpse and emerging with sacred pieces of his being in their greedy maws.

After many minutes, the pies landed atop one other on his desecrated corpse, and began to coalesce. Words fail to convey the horror of such a moment; it was as if they each were stretched like rubber which molded together into a singular being. The form was vaguely human with a monstrous beak, two unblinking eyes, and a pair of small horns protruding from its raised skull. It pointed directly at me and laughed with a sound that made me soil myself. In a deep voice that made the very ground tremble beneath me, it held out its arms and uttered. "Seven for the devil, his own self."

At that point, I blacked out.

The local coroner – Pilgrim was his name – revived me and begged me answer his questions about the incident and the fate that befell Mister Balls, but I could not.

So now you know the truth, Daniel.

My book was intended as a warning, not entertainment.

I deeply regret the confusion caused by my work, and hope you understand the need for its urgent destruction. The power of Hell is very real. I know this because the eyes of Satan have finally landed upon me, and my time has run out. There are now five creatures on my ledge and the sound they make is deafening. The final two are surely imminent. But my maid has now returned with the cakes, I have carved the sigils in my arms, and I have amassed the necessary charms to thwart the Evil one when he comes for my soul.

For God's sake, Daniel. Save yourself. Save everyone. You must destroy the book before

Acknowledgements

This book is dedicated to my musical brothers KA and MD. We went to hell and back together, but I wouldn't change a thing.

Born Again wouldn't exist without editor Kacey Flynn, and our incredible Kickstarter backers: A.□Chan, Aaron Turko, Adriean Koleric, Alexander Haller, Dylan Stafford, Eileen C, G-Man, Jason Copland, Jason Lavochkin, JHMcKeen, Jonas Sværke, Kevin LaPorte, KJ, Konsectatrix, Lawrence Denvir, Lindsey Watson, Mark "boom boom" Bloom, Matt McGrath, Michaela Weber, Nadya, Randy Stone, Richard and Judy Johns, Ryan C, SB Tabor, Stephen Logan, Terry Rainforth, and Warren Frey.

ABOUT THE AUTHOR

JOHN WARD is a Vancouver-based writer, filmmaker, and podcaster. He's the creator and host of the 49 Degrees North Writers Podcast, has made award-winning short films such as *Solus*, and *Linda*, and several comic books including *The Memory Machine*, *Acausal*, *Dark Fragments*, and *Scratcher*. He is a graduate of the UCLA professional program in screenwriting and was previously a recipient of the Telefilm Canada New Voices Award. Before that John was a theoretical physicist holding a PhD in string theory from Queen Mary University of London, and worked at CERN, the University of Iceland, and the University of Victoria. He now lives on the West Coast where he enjoys kayaking, cooking curry, and spending time with his family.

STAY IN TOUCH

Sign up for my monthly newsletter to receive updates, freebies, podcasts, and essays by visiting my personal website www.arbutusfilms.com. While you're there, why not let me know what you thought of the book!

Also by John Ward

Sweet Delicious Candy

Three Tokens for Mammon

Acausal

Scratcher

Offbeats

The Memory Machine

Dark Fragments

The Science of Crowdfunding

9 781738 358045